FLiP-iT-OVER
GUIDES TO TEEN EMOTIONS

A Guys' Guide to

Jealousy

Hal Marcovitz

Enslow Publishers, Inc.
40 Industrial Road
Box 398
Berkeley Heights, NJ 07922
USA

http://www.enslow.com

Library of Congress Cataloging-in-Publication Data

Marcovitz, Hal.
   A guys' guide to jealousy ; A girls' guide to jealousy / Hal Marcovitz
and Gail Snyder.
       p. cm. — (Flip-it-over guides to teen emotions)
   A guys' guide to jealousy ; A girls' guide to jealousy will be
published together in a reversible-book format.
   Includes bibliographical references and index.
   ISBN-13: 978-0-7660-2854-8
   ISBN-10: 0-7660-2854-2
   1. Jealousy—Juvenile literature. 2. Boys—Life skills
guides—Juvenile literature. 3. Girls—Life skills guides—Juvenile
literature. I. Snyder, Gail. II. Title. III. Title: Girls' guide to
jealousy.
   BF575.J4M37 2008
   155.5'1248—dc22

                            2008004692

Printed in the United States of America.

10 9 8 7 6 5 4 3 2 1

Produced by OTTN Publishing, Stockton, N.J.

To Our Readers: We have done our best to make sure all Internet Addresses in this book were active and appropriate when we went to press. However, the author and the publisher have no control over and assume no liability for the material available on those Internet sites or on other Web sites they may link to. Any comments or suggestions can be sent by e-mail to comments@enslow.com or to the address on the title page.

Enslow Publishers, Inc., is committed to printing our books on recycled paper. The paper in every book contains 10% to 30% post-consumer waste (PCW). The cover board on the outside of each book contains 100% PCW. Our goal is to do our part to help young people and the environment too!

Photo Credits: AP Photo/Judi Bottoni, 26; AP Photo/Michael Conroy, 55; AP Photo/Ronen Zilberman, 20; © iStockphoto.com/Dan Brandenburg, 47; © iStockphoto.com/Phil Date, 25; ©iStockphoto.com/ ericsphotography, 52; © iStockphoto.com/Juan Estey, 3, 22; © iStockphoto.com/Miodrag Gajic, 39; © iStockphoto.com/Eileen Hart, 16; © iStockphoto.com/Slobo Mitic, 30; © iStockphoto.com/myshotz, 34; © iStockphoto.com/Kyle Nelson, 56; © iStockphoto.com/Abimelec Olan, 38; © iStockphoto.com/Nuno Silva, 37; © iStockphoto.com/Willie B. Thomas, 17; © 2008 Jupiterimages Corporation, 28; © OTTN Publishing, 35; Used under license from Shutterstock, Inc., 1, 4, 6, 8, 10, 12, 14, 19, 32, 33, 41, 43, 48.

Cover Photo: Used under license from Shutterstock, Inc.

CONTENTS

CHAPTER ONE

What Are Jealousy and Envy?

> Dan and Todd have been friends for many years. When they both tried out for the baseball team, the coach picked Dan as a starter and played him at shortstop. Todd found himself sitting on the bench for most of the games. When he did play, it was usually during the final one or two innings, and always in the outfield. Instead of spending time after practice with Todd, Dan started hanging out with some of the other players on the team. Todd wasn't included. Dan must be the coach's favorite, Todd thought.

Todd was feeling both envy and jealousy. They are not the same, although both can often occur at the same time. Envy refers to the desire to have something that someone else has. Jealousy is the emotional reaction (feelings and thoughts) about losing someone important to you to

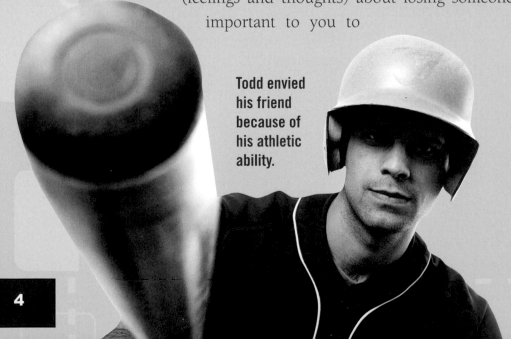

Todd envied his friend because of his athletic ability.

You and Your Emotions

A part of everyone's personality, emotions are a powerful driving force in life. They are hard to define and understand. But what is known is that emotions—which include anger, fear, love, joy, jealousy, and hate—are a normal part of the human system. They are responses to situations and events that trigger bodily changes, motivating you to take some kind of action.

Some studies show that the brain relies more on emotions than on intellect in learning and in making decisions. Being able to identify and understand the emotions in yourself and in others can help you in your relationships with family, friends, and others throughout your life.

another person, or simply the fear and sadness that someone is being taken away by another person. The feeling is often accompanied by other negative emotions, including sadness, anger, fear, and shame, which can be brought on by the thought of such a loss.

A person feels envy when he wants something that someone else possesses. That something could be the latest cell phone, an MP3 player, a celebrity-brand jacket or sneakers, or a baseball glove. But the source of envy can be more than possessions. It can also be the other person's ability or popularity. As much as he liked Dan,

"It is in the character of very few men to honor without envy a friend who has prospered."

—Aeschylus

Differences Between Envy and Jealousy

Envy involves...

Feelings of inferiority

Longing for what someone else has

Resentment

Guilt, if ill will is directed toward a friend

Motivation to improve

Desire to possess another's qualities

Jealousy involves...

Fear of losing someone important to another

Suspicion of unfaithfulness

Anger at a rival

Low self-esteem and sadness over loss

Uncertainty and loneliness

Distrust[1]

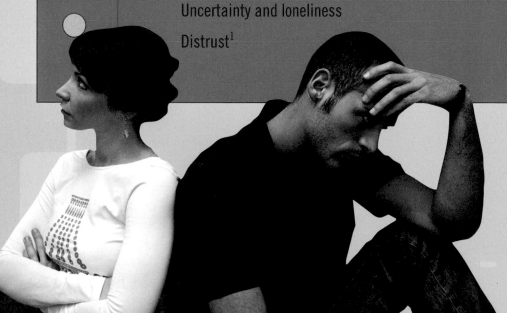

How Do I Know What I'm Feeling?

You feel **envious** when a person has something (a possession, a talent, a relationship) that you want and don't have (or don't believe you have).

You feel **jealous** when you have (or believe you have) a relationship that you don't want to lose or share with others.

Todd envied his friend because he had better athletic ability and a favored position on the team. Todd wished he had his friend's athletic skills as well as his popularity with the coach and other players.

Todd was also feeling jealous because Dan had a new set of friends—the other top players on the team. People who are jealous fear losing a relationship that is important to them. They are often hostile and suspicious toward the people whom they believe are trying to take that relationship away. In Todd's case, because he feared he was losing Dan as a friend, he had a hard time being friendly to the other guys.

Jealousy is often accompanied by the emotions of sadness, shame, anger, and fear. The body has a physical response to these feelings. Some of the most common reactions are an increased heartbeat and an involuntary tensing of muscles.

CHAPTER TWO

Jealousy and Aggression

> Evan stopped short when he saw his girlfriend Madison talking with Jake outside French class. She laughed at something Jake said and smiled at him. Why was she being so nice to Jake? Evan wondered. Was she planning to break up with him? And who did Jake think he was, flirting with his girl? Evan felt like walking up to Jake and shoving him into the wall.

Jealousy and envy are often accompanied by feelings of insecurity. "Jealousy may reflect a person's view of him or herself," says Jo Anne White, professor of education at Temple University. "It's more about how people feel about themselves and whether they're confident about who they are."[1]

People with low self-esteem tend to become jealous easily. The term *self-esteem* refers to the way you feel about yourself. If your self-esteem is low, you are unhappy or annoyed

Evan was jealous because he believed that Madison was flirting with another guy. But was that reaction fair to his girlfriend?

Physical and Emotional Reactions to Jealousy

Some physical reactions are:

Insomnia

Rapid heartbeat

Dizziness

Lack of appetite

Sweaty hands

Shakiness

Some emotional responses are:

Anger

Sadness

Fear and anxiety

Shame and humiliation

Anger and rage

Feelings of helplessness

Feelings of pain

Hurt feelings

with yourself, or you don't think your life is valuable. On the other hand, if you recognize that people love you for who you are, and value your opinions, beliefs, and values, you have high self-esteem.

Anxiety and Jealousy

When people feel jealous and envious, they often experience a lot of anxiety. Anxiety is a mental condition in which people feel dread, fear, and an overwhelming sense that something bad is going to happen to them. Some people experience anxiety attacks in which they feel physically ill—suffering chest pains, stomachaches, lightheadedness, a fast heartbeat, and tense muscles.

Many people struggle with low self-esteem when they are in their teens. During this time of life, it can be especially hard to feel in control and confident in yourself and your abilities. After all, a lot is going on socially, emotionally, and physically: You may be experiencing changing relationships with friends and family. At the same time, you are going through puberty, as your body matures into that of an adult. These physical changes are affecting your moods and the way you see yourself. As you are growing older, you are also having to make new choices in response to demands

Low self-esteem can be a major factor in jealousy and envy.

and pressures from many different directions. The teen years can be a time of great uncertainty.

Having a strong self-image, or confidence in yourself, can help you deal with the changes in your life. But if you lack that confidence and have low self-esteem, you can have negative feelings that affect the way you relate to your family members, friends, and others.

Research has shown that a lack of self-esteem or self-confidence is linked to jealousy and aggression. In a 2005

The Green Emotion?

Have you ever heard someone describe jealousy as "the green-eyed monster"? British playwright William Shakespeare often used the color green when referring to jealousy. He called it the "green sickness" in the play *Antony and Cleopatra* and "green-eyed jealousy" in *The Merchant of Venice*.

The "green-eyed monster" made its first appearance in the play *Othello*, written by Shakespeare around 1603. In the story, Othello is a recently promoted general whose envious aide, Iago, decides to cause Othello's downfall. To do so, he deceives the general into believing his wife, Desdemona, is unfaithful. At the same time, the ungrateful Iago actually warns Othello about the dangers of jealousy, telling him to beware of "the green-eyed monster."

The expression "green with envy" dates from the mid-1800s. To be green with envy means to desire the possessions or accomplishments of someone else.

study, Penn State University researchers used a friendship jealousy questionnaire given to nearly 500 fifth- though ninth-grade students to determine what made them become upset with friends. They asked participants, for example, whether certain classmates were "possessive of their friends" or got "really jealous if you [tried] to be friends with their friend."[2]

Dealing with jealous feelings by avoiding the other person will only make the situation worse.

Aggression is hostile or violent behavior or attitudes directed toward someone else.

The researchers reported that kids who were lonely or who had low self-esteem were more likely to be jealous—to feel that others threatened their friendships. Their typical response to these jealous feelings, the investigators found, was to be aggressive. Some were physically aggressive—they hit or pushed the person they considered to be the source of the problem. However, some teens showed their jealousy by being passively aggressive. That is, they tried to hurt the person they were angry with by isolating him or her from other friends ("We're not inviting him over anymore") or by ignoring the person altogether ("Just don't talk to him").

Rather than letting jealous feelings take over, you can do something about them. Some tips on overcoming the green-eyed monster can be found in chapter 8.

Unhealthy Ways of Dealing with Jealous Feelings

- Putting down or insulting a rival
- Denying that jealousy exists
- Avoiding the person or not speaking to him
- Striking out or using violence

CHAPTER THREE

How Jealous and Envious Are You?

"You must be kidding," Shane looked at his friend Jose in amazement. "You say your girlfriend's old boyfriend is back in town visiting her and you're not bothered? You must not care about her if you're not jealous."

Jose smiled, "I used to get upset when she just looked at someone else. But she made it clear that if she was planning to break up with me, she wouldn't be flirting with other guys. She's honest. How could I not care about someone who's got her act together like that?"

Everyone experiences jealousy and envy at some point in life. However, situations that make one person feel envious or jealous don't have the same effect on someone else. The way you react is unique to you.

Some kids may become strongly jealous when their parents appear to be giving more attention to another member of the family. One guy may be bothered when his girlfriend strikes up a friendship with another boy, while another may not be at all concerned.

If your relationship with your girlfriend is strong, there's no need to feel jealous when she spends time with guy friends.

It can be easy to feel envious of a friend who gets straight A's and barely cracks open a book to study. This can be especially true if you have to prep for hours and hours in order to get a passing grade.

Similarly, feelings of envy can affect one person more than another. In school, did the teacher call on a classmate when you knew the answer? When you played basketball after school, did a teammate score the winning shot? If these situations and others like them bring out feelings of jealousy and envy, you're not alone. Many people feel the same way.

If you are concerned that your feelings of jealousy or envy may be too strong, take the quiz on pages 18–19 to evaluate your reactions to each described situation. Although all of the scenarios described in the quiz might not have happened to you, imagine that they could happen. What would you do in each case?

Are You Too Jealous? Too Envious?

After reading each scenario, give yourself points to indicate if the situation would definitely make you jealous or envious (three points), sometimes (two points), or rarely (one point). If the situation wouldn't bring out any jealous or envious feelings, give yourself zero points.

1. You got your history test back and although you studied hard, you got a B. Your friend got an A, even though he hardly studied at all.

2. Your sister has her own bedroom at home but you have to share a room with your little brother.

3. Your friend gets a job delivering newspapers after school. You apply for a similar job, but the personnel manager tells you the company doesn't need anybody else.

4. For months, you've had a crush on a girl in your class. You finally get up the courage to ask her to the school dance. But she tells you that she is already going with someone else.

5. A girl you like throws a party at her house. Everyone you know seems to have been invited—except you.

6. You go to a Major League baseball game with your friend and he catches a foul ball; after the game, he gets the ball autographed by the player who hit it.

7. You spent a lot of time on your student government campaign, asking people for your vote and hanging posters all over school. Your opponent wins, even though he didn't seem to spend much time and effort campaigning.

8. Your girlfriend got a text message that she doesn't want you to see.

Add up the points. If you scored sixteen to twenty-four points, you probably spend a lot of time stewing over how life is unfair to you. If you scored from eight to sixteen points, you usually manage your jealousy and envy pretty well. However, you could probably benefit by working to boost your self-confidence and self-esteem. If you scored less than eight points, you do a great job of keeping your jealousy and envy from taking over your life.

If your score is high, however, think some more about positive ways to deal with each situation. For example, if your sister gets her own room and you have to share, then perhaps there is nothing you can do about that. But you could still talk with your parents, so they know how you feel—even if the situation can't change. On the other hand, if the newspaper turns you down for a job, wait a few weeks and try again. Chances are the company will have an opening quite soon. Or you could try for a different kind of job instead.

Although it can be hard, try to push yourself past envious feelings. If your friend gets a better grade on a test, what does that mean for you? Feeling envious of his test score will not help you score well on future tests. Instead, use your feelings of envy to motivate yourself. Reevaluate your own study habits. Talk to your teacher. If you work harder, you could score a better grade on your next test. If you think you are too jealous or envious of others, take *positive* steps to change your behavior.

CHAPTER FOUR

Family Competition

As boys, twin brothers Tiki and Ronde Barber were very competitive—especially when it came to football, track, and other sports. "We used to fight all the time," says Tiki. "When we were about 14 or 15, I punched him in the stomach, and I broke my wrist. That was the last time we fought."

Both boys would go on to star in the National Football League—Tiki as a running back for the New York Giants and Ronde as a defensive back for the Tampa Bay Buccaneers. According to Tiki, the two brothers learned how to use their rivalry to help improve as athletes. Says Tiki, "I guess each other's successes would drive us. In high school, he was national champ in the hurdles, and I was like, 'I'm not going to play second fiddle to that.' It pushed me."[1]

The term sibling rivalry refers to the jealousy, competition, and fighting that takes place between brothers and sisters. Siblings often develop rivalries with each other. They may see their brothers or sisters achieve a high grade in school or win an award. Such achievements are usually accompanied by extra

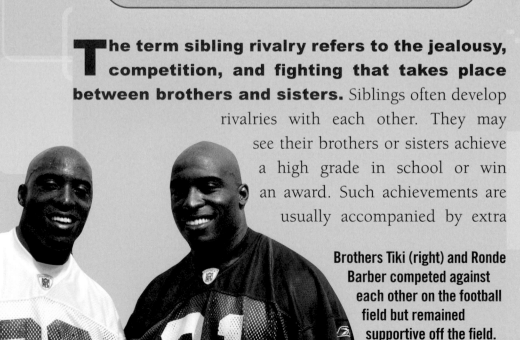

Brothers Tiki (right) and Ronde Barber competed against each other on the football field but remained supportive off the field.

attention from parents, teachers, coaches, or friends. When parents and others lavish attention on one sibling, it can fuel feelings of jealousy in the other sibling.

Sometimes, feelings of rivalry may be affected by birth order. Some researchers believe that the order in which children are born affects their personality. Birth order does affect the way that kids interact in their family. For example, in many families the oldest child is given the most responsibility, while the youngest child may receive less discipline or be treated as the "baby." Differences in treatment by parents—or perceived differences—can be a big factor in the development of sibling rivalry.

One of the most common concerns among brothers and sisters is the feeling that one of them is their parents' favorite.

Birth Order

Some studies have shown that birth order plays a role in personality. Here are some reported birth order characteristics:

Oldest child—high achiever, leader, prone to stress, reliable, follows rules

Middle child—learns to give and take, peacemaker, sometimes feels unloved, avoids conflict

Youngest child—show-off who loves attention, likes people, most spoiled

Only child—mature, shy in groups, articulate, somewhat self-centered[2]

It's hard to take when you think your parents prefer your brother or sister to you—that they are "playing favorites," by allowing your sibling special treatment or giving more gifts.

But are your parents really playing favorites? Keep in mind that you and your siblings are different people with different needs—your little brother may need extra help with homework because math doesn't come easily, while you have never had a problem with it. Your parents may have their reasons for giving more time and attention to the various members of the family. It is also possible that your folks really aren't giving more time and attention—it just seems that way.

Think about the situation before you jump to conclusions. Did your mom say something specific to make you feel she likes your

Brothers and sisters can fall into a routine of arguing with each other all the time—and create a tension that affects everyone in the family.

brother or sister better than you? Was she simply acknowledging some special achievement of your brother or sister? Have your parents never complimented you? Perhaps you are feeling uncertain about how they feel about you. In that case, it's time for a conversation with them. If you think your mother and father are favoring one sibling over another, you need to tell your parents how you feel.

Similarly, if you feel like your folks are unfairly comparing you to your sibling, let them know that the comparisons bother

Why Do Siblings Feel Jealous?

Here are some common situations that can cause jealousy among siblings:

Unequal amounts of parent's attention: "You always go to his basketball games. There's never time to come to my soccer games."

Differences in treatment by parents: "Why do I have so many chores and he doesn't?" "Why do we have the same curfew when I'm three years older than she is?"

Sense of rivalry: "He got a new bike and I didn't get one. Mom and Dad must love him more than they love me." "Big deal, so she got first in the science competition. I could have done the same thing when I was in her grade."

Teasing to get a reaction: "He called me...." "But she called me...first."

Competitive personalities: "I saw it first." "I'm better than you."

If You're Jealous
of Your Sibling

Identify whether you're unhappy with your parent's reaction to your sibling's accomplishments. If that is the case, recognize that you can't help that your parents or other people congratulate your sibling on doing a good job. Try to join in.

Consider whether your sibling's achievements are making you feel badly about yourself. Once you know this, you can then make the effort to focus on being more positive about yourself and your own accomplishments. If you can't do the same thing as well as your brother or sister, you can try to develop your abilities in a different area.

If you're being teased by a competitive sibling for not being as good as he or she is, ignore the behavior. Make it clear that the taunts don't bother you—they'll probably soon stop if you don't react.

you. Maybe they think their comments will motivate you if they say things like, "Your brother always got A's in that class," or "Your sister's room is always so neat. Why isn't yours?" Your parents may not be aware that such comparisons bother you and really aren't motivating you at all. So, have a conversation in which you calmly and clearly tell them, without anger or sarcastic comments, how their comments make you feel. Help your parents understand that comparisons don't help you and if these remarks make you feel bad, your folks need to know.

Regardless of your reasons for feeling envious or jealous of your brother or sister, it is way too easy to fall into the routine of fights and arguments. The desire to be better or the best in the family can lead to put-downs and name-calling, which in turn can lead to pushing, hitting, and shoving. Such conflicts can cause big problems within your family, not only among siblings but also with your parents.

However, conflicts among brothers and sisters don't have to always lead to aggressive behavior. "I've seen how sibling competition can push kids to do their best, or their worst," notes World and Olympic figure-skating coach Craig Maurizi, who has taught many siblings over the years.[3] When brothers and

Fighting with your sibling isn't going to solve anything. Instead, try to find some common ground on which both of you can agree.

Quarterback Sibling Rivalry?

Peyton and Eli Manning are two brothers who are often compared. When they compete against each other, the whole world watches. Peyton plays quarterback for the Indianapolis Colts; Eli quarterbacks the New York Giants. Since Peyton is five years older than Eli, the brothers insist that they never considered each other rivals.

"Peyton's been a great big brother," says Eli. "He's never been pushy about trying to do too much, but if I ever had any questions, he'd do everything he could to help me become a better player."[4]

Peyton (left) and Eli Manning talk during practice.

sisters work together as a team, each can often improve the other's performance by helping develop specific skills.

If you are bothered by the tensions with your brother or sister, and you want to ease them, there are steps you can take. Competitive siblings can improve strained relationships by following these suggestions:

Try not to compare yourself to your sister or brother. Appreciate yourself for the person you are. Recognize you have certain abilities and qualities that no one else has. Although you may share some traits with your brother or sister, you are an individual with your own particular skills and abilities. So don't compare yourself to your sibling. If you must make comparisons, think about how well you did something last year compared to how you did the same thing last week.

Find something good to say. If your brother beat the fastest racer during the last swim meet, congratulate him. Tell your sister you're proud of her ability when she comes in first in the long-distance run. If you both compete in the same sport, recognize that you can help each other out. By practicing together, you can give each other a leg up on others who don't have family competition.

Be willing to compromise. Be willing to give in by letting your brother or sister have his or her own way once in a while. (Compromise means a willingness of both sides to give up something in order to resolve a conflict.)

Play fair, play nice. Fighting matches, loud voices, bragging, and put-downs don't achieve anything. If you are close to physical confrontation, take a break and walk away from the situation for a while. After you have calmed down, try again.

Try to resolve problems. When issues come up, make an extra effort to communicate with your sibling in a

Other Tips for Getting Along with Brothers and Sisters

1. **Spend some time together.** Invite your younger sister to play a board game with you. Ask your older brother to teach you to play the guitar. If you spend more time together, you may be able to understand each other better.

2. **Show an interest in your sibling's hobbies and interests.** Attend his or her sporting events, recitals, or other activities. Share your own hobbies and interests.

3. **If you find yourself becoming irritated over something your sibling has done, take time to cool down.** Walk away from the situation. Take a deep breath and count to ten. Or take several deep breaths and focus on your breathing. When you can think more calmly, come back and talk things out using a calm, quiet voice.

way that will have positive results. Use a calm, quiet voice to explain how you feel. Be willing to negotiate—to reach an agreement through discussion and compromise.

Listen to what your sibling has to say. Let your brother or sister know that you expect the same kind of treatment, too. Once you both understand how the other feels, you'll have a good chance of solving the problem.

When you open up a dialogue, you can share your true feelings. A good way to talk about your issues is with I-messages. These are statements that allow you to tell someone how you feel without blaming him or her for the problem. The box below explains the four parts of an I-message.

Ask for help. If you can't work things out with your sibling, you may have to call in a parent or other trusted adult for advice or to mediate (help bring a conflict to an agreement).

Remember that life is not a competition. Try to rethink your own perspective, too. Your relationship with your brother or sister is not a game and no one's keeping score. Remember, the number of times you or your sibling receives a compliment, gift, or other acknowledgement from your parents doesn't reflect how much they love you.

Using I-messages

Express your feelings in a non-threatening way by using I-messages. An I-message typically has four parts:

1. How you feel ("I felt envious . . .")

2. The action or incident that bothers you (". . . when you and dad bought tickets for the basketball game on a day I couldn't attend . . .")

3. Why you feel the way you do about what happened (". . . because I really wanted to go, too.")

4. How you'd like the situation to be resolved ("Next time you plan to go, I would appreciate it if you would ask me what dates are good.")

CHAPTER FIVE

Envying Others' Possessions

> Peter and his friend Keith both have video game consoles, and whenever they visit each other's homes they enjoy playing games against one another. Keith's parents buy him all the latest games, while Peter's parents think their son should pay for video games himself. Keith owns hundreds of games, while Peter has been able to afford only a couple. He wishes his parents would spend money on him like Keith's parents do.

Envy doesn't usually occur over something you need, but rather something you want. Wanting things is a big part of the consumer culture of today. It has become too easy to feel that owning the latest celebrity

When your friend has more advanced electronic devices than you, do you feel envious?

basketball sneakers, hottest video game, or sports jersey is all you need to make you happy.

A consumer culture. You are constantly being besieged with commercial messages from companies trying to convince you to buy their products. Everywhere you look—on the TV or Internet, over the radio, on billboards, in newspapers or magazines—companies and celebrities warn you that if you don't buy their clothes, sneakers, cell phones, or video games, you'll miss out on the good things of life. Many people develop feelings of being inadequate simply because they don't have what everyone else has.

It can be very hard to feel a part of the group when "everyone else" has the latest pair of running shoes, sports team jacket, or electronic device. Sometimes, envy of what another guy owns—such as expensive clothing or shoes—has led to assault. In a handful of cases, murders have been committed over a pair of basketball sneakers, sports jerseys, or MP3 players.

So what do you do if someone has something you want? Well, you can brood about it, thinking dark thoughts of envy toward the kid with the great jacket or massive video game

Redirecting Envy

At the first sign that you are feeling envy, you need to do something to redirect the feeling. Otherwise your envy is likely to keep growing stronger. When you obsess over what you don't have, you are digging a hole deeper, rather than climbing out of it.

Techno-Envy

A report by the Urban Institute, a Washington, D.C.-based research organization, argues that a rise in violent crime since 2004 can be linked to the growing popularity of the MP3 player. The article noted that the increase in robbery has been greatest among juvenile offenders. Another story in the *New York Times* reported the rise of crime in city subways which most often involved teenagers robbed of their iPods and cell phones.[1] In some cases, teens have killed other teens during such robberies.

Massachusetts Institute of Technology professor Henry Jenkins says the thefts are a result of "techno-envy."[2] He explains that not everyone can afford to buy such costly technology. But expensive cell phones and MP3 players are, in Jenkins' words, "considered essential to being a young person."[3] So techno-envy can result in an increase of thefts as those without the latest devices steal from those who have them.

collection. Or you can feel angry toward his parents, for buying him whatever he wants. Or you could stop a moment and focus your thoughts on what is really bothering you—the particular item or items that sparked your envy in the first place.

Ask yourself: Do I really need this <u>fill in the blank</u>? If so, why do I want it? Will I want it three months from now? A year from now? Is it worth the cost? After giving it some thought, you may decide that you really don't want the <u>fill in the blank</u> that much—that there are other things of more importance to you.

However, if the answer to the last three questions is "yes," then you need to start thinking about how you could go about getting it. In other words, use your envy in a positive way—to motivate you to get what you want. Perhaps you can take a part-time job, start up a lawn-mowing business, or offer to do work for your neighbors to earn extra money. You may find that by the time you've earned the money to buy the item, you no longer want it. But with the cash in hand, you'll have the knowledge that you could buy it if you really wanted to.

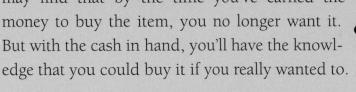

If you just have to get that MP3 player or video game system, figure out a way to earn the money to buy it.

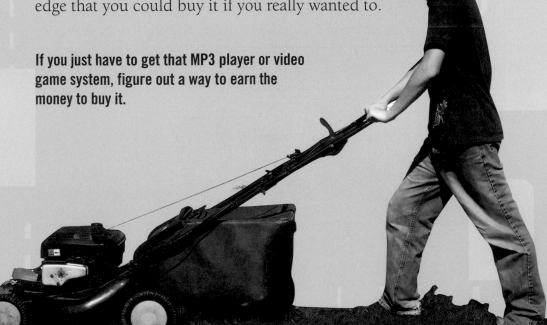

CHAPTER SIX

When You're Jealous of Friends

When Tyler reminded his friends Zach and Luis about his party on Friday night, they both told him they couldn't make it. "We already told Seth we'd be at his place. There's going to be a bunch of other guys there playing video games," Zach said. "He has all these consoles so ten guys can play at the same time."

"What do you mean? You forgot about my party?" Tyler demanded angrily. He didn't really know Seth—who was new to the school. But he had already decided he didn't like him.

It's easy to feel jealous when your friends decide to spend time with others when you were counting on them to be there for you. It can also be hard to know what to do when a friend is unhappy with you just because you decided to hang out with another friend. Jealousy can often cause conflicts among

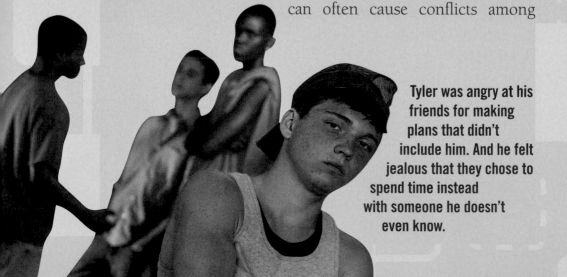

Tyler was angry at his friends for making plans that didn't include him. And he felt jealous that they chose to spend time instead with someone he doesn't even know.

Dealing with the Emotions of Jealousy and Envy

Deal with the negative emotions that accompany jealousy by identifying and estimating how much each of these emotions affects you. For example, you may calculate that you are feeling 50 percent angry, 30 percent fearful, and 20 percent powerless. Once you've identified your feelings, deal with the biggest negative emotion first. If you think anger is the biggest issue, focus on controlling that anger first.

One way to analyze your feelings of jealousy:

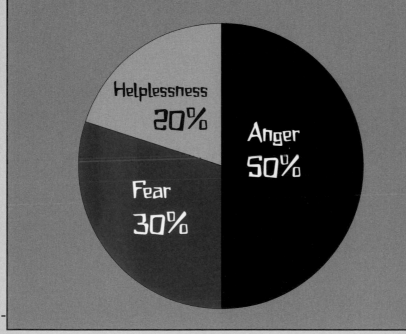

Helplessness 20%

Anger 50%

Fear 30%

friends, especially when one demands that you choose one of them over another.

As each year goes by in your life, you are meeting new people and having the opportunity to make new friends. You are

Four Ways Teens Deal with Jealous Feelings

Researchers asked ninth graders if they had felt neglected or been neglected by a friend as a result of the friend dating. More than 60 percent said yes. Many teens reported strong feelings of jealousy, as well as a good deal of anger and hurt, because of feeling left out. About one-third of the boys in the study reported feeling excluded by a best friend because he was dating someone.

The students were asked what they would do in such situations. Researchers placed their responses into the following four categories:

Voice: "Talk to your friend about it."

Exit: "She should leave the friend." "He should just move on and get another friend." "Give her the cold shoulder."

Loyalty: "He must accept that he'll always be your best friend, even if he is ignoring you right now."

Disregard: "There is nothing you can do." "Just forget it."

However, most participants in the study recommended "Voice" as the best way to act when a friend seems neglectful. They said that it was far better to "talk things out," rather than abandon the friendship or ignore the problem.[1]

developing new interests—in sports, music, clubs, volunteer opportunities, and many other kinds of activities. As the circle of people you get to know grows wider, you may find that you prefer doing stuff with the people who share your new interests.

Things can become complicated when a girlfriend enters the mix. If she doesn't like your friends, or they don't like her, arguments can result.

When You're Jealous of Friends

Tips for Keeping Jealousy and Envy Out of Friendships

Don't betray a confidence. Trust is an important part of friendship. If your friend tells you a secret, don't tell others.

Be supportive. If a friend asks for your opinion, be honest. It is okay to tell a friend when you think he or she is making a mistake. But before you criticize your friend, think about your reasons. Do you mean well, or are you feeling envious?

Acknowledge success. You may become jealous when your friend wins the wrestling tournament while you were eliminated in the first round. But a strong person can put that jealousy aside and celebrate his friend's success.[2]

Don't yell! Talk to your friend if she's complaining that you're spending too much time with your other friends.

However, good friends don't dump their old friends every time they meet someone new. They try to be aware that a friend's feelings may be hurt when they spend less time hanging out. A good friend works to avoid any jealous feelings by including old friends in activities with new ones.

It can get even trickier when the new friend is a girlfriend. Your buddies may feel left out, especially if you start dating before they do. They may be bothered when you spend more time with her than with them. And your girlfriend may not be interested in joining your other friends when you go to the movies or out for pizza. In fact, she may not even like them or want you to spend any time with them.

So what do you do? If you'd rather keep a romantic relationship separate from your other relationships, the best thing to do is to try to balance the amount of time you spend with those people. You might set up a regular date night and a time you want to just hang out with the guys.

CHAPTER SEVEN

Dating and Jealousy

> Kevin thought Kris was the most beautiful girl at school. When he finally got up the courage to ask her for a date, he was shocked that she said yes. Soon they were seeing each other every weekend.
>
> Soon Kevin became aware of how other boys looked at Kris. At first, he felt proud that he was dating the best-looking girl in school, but soon he was struggling with pangs of jealousy. Any time he saw another boy look at Kris, he wanted to punch the guy in the nose. Whenever he found her talking to another guy, Kevin would grab Kris's arm and pull her away.

While a little jealousy can be a good thing in a relationship, feeling too jealous is unhealthy when both people don't trust one another and have respect for each other's feelings. When Kevin started noticing how other boys looked at his girlfriend, he feared losing something very important to him—his relationship with Kris. His jealousy resulted in a range of emotions. He felt anger and fear at the thought that someone else could take Kris away from him. He was disappointed that she would dare to look at another guy. And he felt suspicious of her behavior: Why did she keep flirting with these other

Jealousy eats away at the one thing that holds a relationship together: Trust.

Avoid jealous feelings by talking about what is bothering you.

guys? And why were other guys flirting with her? She had to be encouraging them.

You may also find yourself struggling with your own jealous feelings over the relationship with your girlfriend. Say you see her in the hallway at school having a conversation with some other guy you don't know. Suddenly your heart is pounding and your hands are sweating, and you feel somewhat sick. You're feeling jealous, and these feelings are perfectly normal. Listen to them. They indicate that you feel threatened, or rather, that you believe your relationship is threatened.

There are many ways you could react to your jealous feelings. You could fly into a rage by shouting at your girlfriend and making a scene. Or you could turn away, and avoid the situation, keeping your upset feelings inside. Or you could

Good Relationships Don't Include Jealousy

If you are having problems with jealous feelings in a relationship, keep in mind the following seven keys to keeping things good between the two of you:

Respect. Mutual respect is a key part of any relationship. Don't force her to do something that goes against her values and beliefs; similarly, let her know if her expectations go against your own.

Trust. Even when jealous feelings arise, you can manage your reactions by believing the other person is telling the truth.

Honesty. Don't lie. It's tough to have trust when one of you isn't being honest.

Support. Be there for each other—with a shoulder to cry on when life is tough and to celebrate with during the good times.

Fairness and equality. You take turns, whether choosing which new movie to see or whose friends to hang out with. You are both willing to compromise.

Separate identities. Keep up with hobbies, friends, and interests. Neither of you should have to pretend to like something you don't, or give up seeing your friends, or drop out of activities you love.

Good communication. You are troubled, but when your girlfriend asks you about it you say, "Nothing is wrong." Learn to communicate honestly and openly with your girlfriend. Avoid miscommunication.[1]

figure out a way to cope. That is, you could use your feelings of jealousy to make your relationship stronger.

A little jealousy in a dating relationship can actually be a good thing if you recognize it as a signal that something needs work. The best way to manage your feelings is by talking about what feels wrong with the person most directly able to do something about it—your girlfriend. Maybe she *was* flirting with someone else. But it is also possible that she was simply talking with a friend.

In a calm, collected way, you need to let her know why the situation made you feel jealous. Then listen, without interrupting, to what she has to say. Remember, open communication is the best way to ensure your relationship stays strong. Redirect feelings of jealousy to efforts to improve your relationship.

Using jealousy to manipulate. Like Kevin, boys can feel jealous if they *even think* their girlfriend is interested in other boys. When *Teen People* magazine asked teenage boys about what makes them jealous, most said they get jealous when their girlfriends

Is she trying to make you jealous by flirting on the phone?

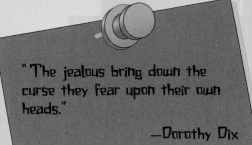

spend time with other boys. One teen noted that he knew girls who have intentionally tried to make him jealous. "I'm not a jealous person," said the teen, "but it irks me when a girl intentionally tries to make me jealous by talking about some guy a lot."[2]

Trying to make the other person in a relationship jealous on purpose is manipulating the relationship. In some cases, it may be the girl who is jealous. Because she is uncertain about where she stands with her boyfriend, she flirts with other guys on purpose. She may be worried that he wants to date other girls. So to keep his attention, she tries to make him jealous. Keep in mind that this kind of behavior, of intentionally causing someone to feel painful, jealous feelings, reflects a relationship in trouble.

Sometimes a girl may show her jealousy by being possessive. If she wants to know who you've been talking to, what you do after school, why you don't call her every night—

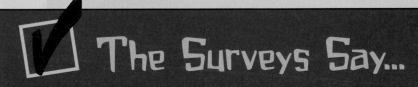

The Surveys Say...

A survey conducted in 2006 of thirteen- to eighteen-year-olds found that 64 percent of teens in dating relationships were with someone who "acted really jealous and asked where they were all the time." More than half of teens in relationships—61 percent—said they've had a boyfriend or girlfriend who made them feel bad or embarrassed about themselves, due to verbal, emotional, and physical threats.[3]

chances are she's jealous of anyone else you may be with. If you think your girlfriend is intentionally trying to make you jealous or that she is acting overly possessive, you may want to reevaluate your relationship. Talk to her. Let her know how you feel and how her behavior is affecting you. If nothing changes, it would appear that she isn't able to respect your feelings. You might be better off without her.

Irrational jealousy. The lack of trust in a relationship can sometimes cause one person—or both—to need constant reassurance that he or she is number one. That demand for reassurance may mean the jealous person goes to extremes in always wanting to know where the other person is and what he or she is doing. For example, if Kevin's girlfriend isn't answering her phone, he could believe that she is busy with something else or has a good reason for being unable to text message in response. But if his first thought is that she's not answering because she's hanging out with another guy, he is showing a complete lack of trust in her and in their relationship. When a guy doesn't have evidence that his girlfriend is lying to him, but still accuses her of cheating on him, he is suffering from irrational jealousy.

Irrational jealousy is extreme, long-lasting jealousy in which a person becomes obsessed with the object of his affection. He typically becomes overly controlling and possessive in their relationship, telling his girlfriend what to wear, preventing her from spending free time with friends, and insisting that she

A person with irrational jealousy can be physically sick with fear over the possibility of losing a relationship, even though his actions are actually destroying it.

Is Your Friend Showing Early Warning Signs of Irrational Jealousy?

- He blames others for his problems.

- When he gets angry, he often hits things or breaks things.

- If he has a girlfriend, he is constantly checking up on her.

- He always wants to be in charge, especially if he has a girlfriend. He likes to be the one who decides which movie to see or where to eat.

- He may be cruel to animals or try to push others around, especially kids who are smaller or younger.

- His anger is explosive.

- There are times when he likes to be by himself and doesn't appreciate your friendship.

- He is inflexible. In other words, once he makes up his mind he won't change it. And it is hard to convince him to do something he doesn't want to do.

- He has low self-esteem.

- He may abuse illegal substances.

- If he gets into an argument with you, he may shove you or punch you to get you to agree with him.

- His expectations may be unrealistic. If he fails, he may grow depressed even though he may have tried to accomplish something that was beyond his ability.

- He resorts to foul language and name-calling, especially during an argument.[4]

check in with him constantly (by text messaging on her cell phone, for example). If she tries to assert herself or argue with his restrictions, he may explode with anger and become violent.

With irrational jealousy, it is often the girl who can be in real physical danger if her boyfriend is overly possessive and controlling. Fights and arguments over who she was with and what she was doing can lead to dating violence. She may be emotionally abused—by teasing, name-calling, ridiculing, and threats. Or she could be physically abused by being grabbed, slapped, or even choked. In some cases, dating violence may include sexual abuse as well.

One study has shown that things like television programs, advertising, and music videos send the message that young men have the "right" to control their girlfriends and that masculinity involves being physically aggressive.[5] As a result some guys

Fear of losing a relationship can happen with normal jealousy. Irrational jealousy typically involves that fear combined with controlling and even abusive behavior.

come to believe they are supposed to control relationships and that it is okay to treat women disrespectfully.

If you have a friend who is treating a girlfriend in a rough way, you need to let him know that his behavior is not right. Most guys who are possessive or controlling don't think of themselves as being abusive or violent in their relationship. You can help a friend by letting him know if you believe his jealousy is irrational and that his behavior bothers you. Encourage him to get help, perhaps from a coach or other trusted adult, or through a local counseling program or other community resource. Offer to go with him if he wants support.

If you are concerned about a friend, talk to her to see how you can help.

You could also make him aware of other ways to help him deal with his problem. Another source of help would be a local

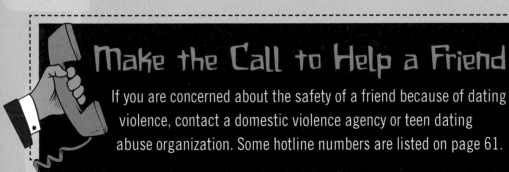

Make the Call to Help a Friend

If you are concerned about the safety of a friend because of dating violence, contact a domestic violence agency or teen dating abuse organization. Some hotline numbers are listed on page 61.

Friends and Abuse

When talking to a friend who might be abused:

- Listen to what she has to say, and don't be judgmental.

- Let her know you are there for her whenever she needs to talk, and that you are worried about her.

- Let her know that you won't tell anyone she doesn't want you to about her situation—and then keep your word (unless you fear for her physical safety).

- Be specific about why you are concerned—"I felt bad when I saw him insult you in front of all of us. He doesn't have the right to treat you that way. What did you think about it?" Let her know about behavior you have seen and how it made you feel.

- Help her locate information and resources on abuse.

- Find someone knowledgeable about abuse whom she can talk to, and volunteer to go with her.

- If she doesn't want to leave or is afraid to do so, remain supportive. Let her know you'll be there for her whenever she needs you.[6]

or national domestic violence hotline. The National Teen Dating Abuse Helpline is a national organization that provides confidential twenty-four-hour assistance to teens. Contact information for telephone hotlines can be found on page 61.

Extreme jealousy should be treated by a mental health professional such as a counselor or psychologist. He or she will provide therapy (treatment) to help your friend learn to deal with dangerous behavior that can come with irrational jealousy.

CHAPTER EIGHT

Controlling Feelings of Envy and Jealousy

Be willing to change. If you think that your jealousy and envy are ruining your friendships and making your life miserable, you can do something about it. But you have to make the effort.

Dealing with envy. If you feel envious of Jamal because he has a great slam dunk or of Casey because her folks just bought her the latest cell phone, you need to pause and think. Don't focus on how angry or envious you feel about Jamal and Casey. Focus instead on the particular thing that they have—the special talent or specific item—that is causing your envy. Then ask yourself, is this talent or is this item something that I really need to have? Or is it simply something I really want to have?

If you can't get past the feeling that you must have it, ask yourself, how can I go about getting it? Perhaps you can practice harder and gain the skills to be as good as Jamal. Or you could work hard at a part-time job and earn the money to buy a cell phone like Casey's. But it is also possible that you won't get as good as Jamal or make enough money to get that phone. Instead, you need to come to terms with yourself and who you are. Recognize that everyone has different interests, skills, abilities, and

"Jealousy is simply and clearly the fear that you do not have value. ... If you cannot love yourself, you will not believe that you are loved."

—Jennifer James

Tips for Managing Feelings of Envy and Jealousy

Don't compare yourself to others. If you received a poor grade on the math test, recognize that the grade your friend received will have no effect on your performance. Similarly, if you received a high grade, don't check around the classroom to see whether anybody else did as well as you. Measure yourself not against others but against yourself. If you score a B on your math test, ask yourself what you have to do to score an A the next time.

Learn from the past. Do other people say you are a jealous person? Have you had problems with jealousy in previous friendships and relationships? If so, you know you need to work on managing these feelings.

Get another opinion. Ask a friend if he or she thinks you are being over the top with your requests in your friendship. Get another perspective on whether your behavior around your girlfriend is a cause of problems in your relationship.

Realize you can't control others. If you are dating a girl and she breaks your movie date for Saturday night, recognize that she probably has a good reason. Her family may have made last-minute plans to travel out of town, or she may figure she needs extra time to finish up a school assignment. Give her space and accept that things won't always go your way.

Be aware of your emotions. There is no need to fly into a rage when others do better than you or achieve the recognition you hoped for. Your unhappy or angry feelings are not their fault, but your own choice. You can control jealousy by choosing to respond in other ways: for example, by being happy for them or by simply ignoring their success.

You shouldn't give up your friendships because of a jealous friend or significant other.

talents. Instead of trying to be like someone else, you will be better off in the long run if you don't focus on what you don't have or who you aren't. Instead, try to focus on what you do have and what you're good at.

In fact, you may have talents in areas you haven't yet explored. Instead of obsessing over things you can't do, try out some new activities. Develop new skills. You may find that you have talents you didn't know about before.

Dealing with jealousy. Similarly, if you find yourself becoming jealous because a friend has less time to spend with you, or a girlfriend has turned you down for a date, stop and examine your feelings. You need to recognize that jealousy has a purpose, says Erik Fisher, who wrote *The Art of Managing Everyday Conflict*: "All emotions, even jealousy, are trying to tell us something about ourselves," he writes. Fisher believes that

When Others Are Jealous of You

If you think your friends are feeling jealous of you, find out why and then do something about it. For example, perhaps you have been invited to a party, and your friends haven't been invited. Instead of ignoring their feelings, find out if you can invite them to come as your guests (as long as it is okay with the host). Getting your friends to share in your experiences is a good way to decrease their feelings of envy and jealousy.

However, if you know that the number of guests is limited, be upfront with your friends. Tell them you're planning to go, but that you'll see them later that night. Or you could suggest that you all get together the next night. This way, you're letting them know your friendship with them is important to you.

If you believe others are envious of you because of your abilities, talents, or accomplishments, be sensitive to how you sound when you talk about what you are doing. To lessen any feelings of ill will, don't brag about yourself. You can show leadership without boasting about your successes. Try to be an example that others can learn from.

jealousy reflects the fear of losing power, but "[w]hen we find out what we're missing in ourselves, that fear goes away."[1]

Do you feel like Doug is no longer your friend because he's going hiking with Miguel and Max this weekend,

Rather than dwelling on feelings of jealousy, recognize that the real problem is you're not sure about your relationship.

instead of hanging out with you? Maybe Kayla wants to celebrate her girlfriend's birthday with a movie out this Saturday, instead of watching television with you. Because the people important to you don't always want to be with you doesn't necessary mean your relationship is on the rocks.

Think about what's really going on. Maybe you are being unrealistic in expecting your friends to spend all their time with you. But if you feel bad about your relationship—whether with friends or with someone you really care about, you need to talk about it. Let the other person in your relationship understand if you don't feel happy about how you're being treated. You're wondering if there is a problem and you would like to make things better. Make sure you find out how he or she feels, too.

From time to time your friends are probably going to do better in school than you. They may perform better on the baseball field, win praise that you feel you deserve, or own clothes that you would love to have. They may date the girl you wanted to ask out or attend parties where you're not

As soon as you recognize you are feeling potentially negative emotions, do something positive about them. Let them motivate yourself to do something better or to figure out how to get something you want.

NASCAR Envy

Jeff Gordon was racing on the NASCAR circuit when nineteen years old—an early age for the sport. Since he got his start so young, Gordon was envied by older drivers, who wondered how he could so quickly advance in the sport. Many of the older drivers were hostile to Gordon.

"I was used to the names—kid, boy, squirt, even a few punks—but I always laughed them off," Gordon says. "In every car and every league I'd ever raced in, I was always the youngest and the smallest. I experienced a lot of jealousy and resentment at every level."[2]

Gordon dealt with the harsh feelings by committing himself to his sport. He worked harder and raced faster than the other competitors. He became the youngest driver in history to win the NASCAR championship; the youngest driver to win the sport's biggest race, the Daytona 500; and the youngest driver to win fifty races. By the time Gordon became a top driver in NASCAR, the jealousy and envy shown by others had largely been replaced by admiration.

invited. You'll be envious and jealous. And those feelings are okay. In fact, they are perfectly normal.

Remember, when you feel confident about yourself, you're less likely to feel jealous in relationships. To avoid insecure feelings in your relationships with family, friends, and others, work on building up your own confidence. Even if you're feeling shy or unsure of yourself right now, recognize that there

One way to bolster your self-esteem is to make a list of things you do well.

have been many times in your life when you were very confident and sure of yourself. Remember, for example, how you felt the first time you mastered how to ride a bicycle, sink a basketball, or win a video game.

Next, make a list of all the things you are good at: for example, maybe you enjoy listening and helping out others, or math comes easy to you, or you're a good artist. Then add more entries to your list: your achievements and accomplishments. These can include compliments from friends, as well as any academic, music, or sports awards you may have received during your lifetime. After you finish your list, take a look at it. The final account may give you some confidence in yourself, especially when you realize the person you've just described on this list has accomplished a lot.

Receiving praise from others is another way to boost your confidence and self-esteem. But did you know that the same thing happens for your friends when you give them positive comments whenever they try something new? If you help boost the confidence and self-esteem of your friends by telling them that they are doing a good job, it is likely they will also return the favor.

Life may still seem unfair at times. However, instead of sitting at home and simmering in a stew of jealousy, work on thinking positively about yourself and others so you can avoid negative feelings. When you're feeling better about yourself, you'll find you're not so easily overwhelmed by the green-eyed monster. And when you can control that monster, you prevent it from harming your relationships with family, friends, and others who are important to you.

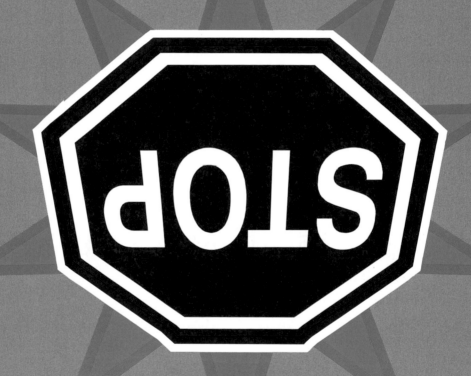

GIRLS!

STOP

Boring Guys' Stuff From This Point On!

GUYS!

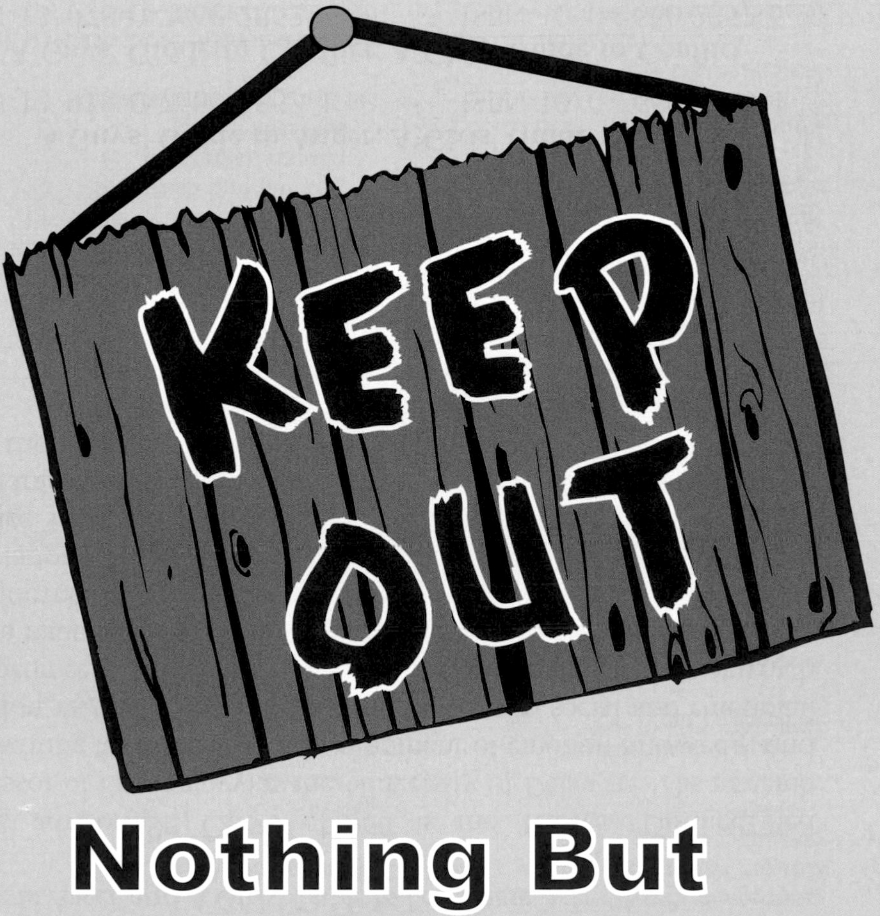

Nothing But Girl Talk Ahead– You've Been Warned!